Alien

by

Tony Bradman

For Tom, who loves this kind of stuff
– just like me!

First American edition published in 2012 by Stoke Books,
an imprint of Barrington Stoke Ltd
18 Walker Street, Edinburgh, United Kingdom, EH3 7LP

www.stokebooks.com

Copyright ©2006 Tony Bradman
Illustrations © Julie-ann Murray

A catalog record for this book is available from
the US Library of Congress

Distributed in the United States and Canada by Lerner Publisher
Services, a division of Lerner Publishing Group, Inc.
241 First Avenue North, Minneapolis, MN 55401
www.lernerbooks.com.

ISBN 978-1-78112-025-5

Printed in China

Contents

1   Dead Kids   1

2   Feeling Jumpy   10

3   Ambush!   18

4   Cornered!   27

5   A Huge Trick   36

6   Healing Time   45

Chapter 1
Dead Kids

It was dark, but there was a moon.

The ruins in front of them glowed blue.

Jake raised his hand to halt his squad of

fighters.

The glow can mean only one thing, he thought. Krell weapons have been used here, and not long ago. Alien eyes may be fixed on the squad right now, alien fingers on triggers ...

"Fan out and take cover," Jake said in a low voice. "Tiny, you're with me!"

Jake ducked behind a wall and watched the squad following his orders quickly and without a sound. Ten rough soldiers in helmets and body armor,

their faces painted green and black. His

squad, ready to fight even when they

were worn out.

Not bad for a bunch of kids, thought

Jake. *But then I'm just a kid too.*

"Should I log on, Jake?" said Tiny,

squatting down beside him.

Jake looked at his Comms Man. His real name was Gary, but the squad called him Tiny because he was so big. The battered old laptop Tiny pulled from his backpack seemed like a toy in his hands. Not many kids made it to Tiny's size by the time they were 12. *Not many kids make it to the age of 12 at all these days*, thought Jake. *I'm the oldest. How the heck did I make it to 14? Most of the squad are ten or 11. One of them is only*

nine.

"Yeah, Tiny," Jake sighed. "Time for

another little chat with HQ."

Tiny's fingers clicked over the

laptop's keys, inputting the security code

and their squad number. A face came up

on screen, an old man with silver hair

and cold blue eyes.

"Report, Squad Leader," said the man. "What's going on out there?"

"It looks like the enemy has been up to something in Sector 3, sir," said Jake. "Can I call in extra troops?"

"No, you can't," snapped the old man. "You must attack."

"But sir, we don't know how strong the enemy force is," said Jake. "And we're very tired. We've been on patrol

for days now ..."

"We're all tired," said the old man.

"But this is a war for the survival of the

human race. You can rest when we've

won. Is that clear?"

"Quite clear, sir," said Jake with a

shrug, and gave the salute. "Just do your

job, Squad Leader," said the old man.

"Over and out."

Tiny logged off and closed the laptop.

He looked at Jake and waited.

I know what he's thinking, thought

Jake. *He's hoping I won't obey orders,*

that I'll tell the squad to pull back while

we still can. That's what I should do.

I've seen too much blood, too many dead

kids. It's OK for The Old Ones. They sit

safe in their deep bunkers while us kids

do the dying. I'd give anything to save

the kids in my squad. But how can I?

"So what's the plan, Jake?" said Tiny.

"What are we going to do?"

"We don't have a choice, Tiny," said

Jake. "We're going to attack."

Chapter 2
Feeling Jumpy

Jake called the squad over. They

huddled around him in the moonlight,

their eyes white in their dark faces.

"OK, listen up, guys," said Jake.

"Same as usual. Katie, Shofiq and Joe, you take the right flank. Sarah, Dan and Alfie, you're on the left. Maria, Polly and Wicksy, you're in the middle with Tiny."

"Any idea how many Krell are in there?" said Sarah.

Good question, Sarah, thought Jake. *She'll make Squad Leader one day. After I'm dead …*

"Could be just a patrol, like us," Jake said. "Could be more. The only way we'll find out is by going in."

"The more the merrier," said Alfie. He checked the energy level in his rifle and grinned. "Bring on the whole Krell army, that's what I say."

The others laughed. *They're feeling jumpy,* thought Jake. *They know that what lies ahead might be pain and death and some of them not coming back. But*

they'll follow me if I ask them.

"And what about you, Jake?" Tiny

asked. "Where will you be?"

"Out front, as always," said Jake. "It's

a tough job, but someone's got to do it."

One or two of them began to laugh again.

But not all of them.

"OK, people," Jake said. "Let's go to work. And stay cool."

"Yeah, and you take it easy too, Jake," said Tiny. Their eyes met.

"I'll be fine, Tiny," said Jake, smiling. "Don't you worry about me."

Jake pulled down his helmet over his face ... and left the cover of the wall. He ran across open ground, keeping low. He made for a big ruin, his laser rifle up and ready. The squad fanned out on either side and behind him. He reached the ruin and went around it.

There was more open space beyond. Jake saw it was a playground. So the ruin must have been a school once ...

That's where we should be, thought Jake. *In a class learning stuff, or out playing games. I can't remember being at school. I was only there for a year before the Krell came and the Dark Time started. I had a mom and dad then, a brother and sister...*

Jake slipped into a shadow. His mind filled with memories – bad things happening, hiding out alone, being found and trained to fight back.

The Old Ones always say they have to use kids, he thought. *Almost all the adults who could fight are dead by now.*

I wonder how the war started in the first

place, why the Krell came here. Are they

as evil as The Old Ones say? This can't

go on much longer. Soon there won't be

any kids left ...

"Jake, watch out!" Tiny yelled
suddenly. "They're behind you!"

There was a blue flash, and Jake felt
a burning pain in his arm.

Chapter 3
Ambush!

Jake spun around and dived behind the nearest pile of rubble. *Oh no*, he thought. *I must have led us into an ambush after all.*

The dark night was filled with crackling laser beams, blue from the Krell, white from his squad. There were screams and yells, human and alien. Jake checked his arm. He had been hit. His sleeve was smoking where the Krell beam had ripped through it, and he was bleeding. But it didn't look like he'd been hurt too badly.

I don't have time to worry about it, he thought. *I can use the arm, and that means I can still fight.* He peered past the rubble ... and a blue beam blasted into it, spraying his face with dust and grit. He pulled back and lay flat for a second, while he got his breath back. Then he rolled to the other side of the rubble and looked out again. He was more careful this time.

There was no blue beam. The Krell

fire was aimed at his squad now.

They're being squeezed hard from both

flanks, Jake thought.

Suddenly he went cold all over.

Somehow the Krell had gotten between

him and the squad. He was cut off and

on his own. So that meant the Krell

could take him out whenever they

wanted.

Not if I can help it, thought Jake. *I'll have to go further into the ruins.*

Then maybe I can work my way around, join up with the squad again. I hope no one else has been hit yet ...

Jake crawled away from the rubble into deeper shadow. He looked back across the playground. The fire-fight seemed to be getting worse. *There's nothing else I can do*, he thought. *I'll have to stick to my plan.*

He turned and ran out of the playground, keeping low. Dark shapes loomed up around him. *Just the same old burnt-out cars and ruins*, he thought. *So why does it feel spookier than normal? Maybe lots of people died here. Maybe their ghosts are watching me ...*

He stopped to think which way he should go. *Left or right? It doesn't really matter.*

It was oddly still away from the fire-fight, too. So still that he could hear footsteps ... Jake froze. The hairs prickled on the back of his neck.

I'm being followed, he thought. *The Krell must have spotted me.*

Jake jumped over a low wall and hid behind it. He scanned the darkness, for any sign of movement, or the glow of an alien weapon. *Wait ...* he thought. *Is that something, or are my eyes just playing tricks?*

Suddenly a blue beam shot out of the night and sizzled past Jake's ear. He fired back, but another blue beam blasted into the top of the wall, then another. Jake turned and fled, looking

for more cover.

He could hear footsteps in the ruins

behind him.

Chapter 4
Cornered!

Jake ran. He slipped and stumbled.

His arm was starting to hurt much more,

and he could feel warm blood trickling

down inside his sleeve. Soon his breath

was coming in gasps. He didn't think he

could keep going.

He stopped by the stump of a

lamppost. A blue blast sizzled into it.

Damn, he thought. *They're getting*

too close. He looked around in despair.

He saw a house nearby, its door open.

Got to hide, he thought and ducked

inside. *Maybe they'll go past and I can*

go back the way I came ... But the hall

was blocked with rubble. The stairs were

his only way to a hiding place.

Jake took them two at a time ... then

tripped at the top and fell on the arm

that had been shot. He cried out with

pain and dropped his rifle. He felt for it

in the dark – but he heard footsteps in

the street, and froze for a second. There

was silence ... then the footsteps came

closer. Jake dragged himself into one of

the rooms as silently as he could.

There was a big hole where a window

had been. Moonlight was pouring in,

leaving only the corners of the room in

the dark. Jake crawled over to a corner

far from the door and sat there, his back

against the wall. *I'm trapped*, he

thought. *But I won't die without a fight.*

He pulled out his combat knife. Pain
shot down his arm, and he winced.

He listened, aware of every sound.
And there were the footsteps again.

Inside the house now, thought Jake.
*They're checking it out ... maybe they'll
just take a quick look around and move
on. Maybe they'll think I kept running.*
A stair creaked, a second, a third. *No*

such luck, thought Jake. He gripped the

hilt of his knife. *Here they come ...*

The footsteps were on the landing.

Jake pulled himself to his feet as a dark

shape filled the doorway. It was a Krell

warrior. The moonlight glinted on the

alien body armor and weapon. Krell

helmets always hid their faces. *I'm glad*

about that, he thought. *I don't want the*

last thing I ever see to be a look of

hate ...

Jake raised his knife and got ready to attack, his body tense, his eyes fixed on the alien's weapon. The alien seemed to take aim, and Jake waited for the blue flash, the agony as the laser beam sliced and diced him. But nothing happened. The warrior stood there, silent and still. Jake suddenly felt very angry.

"Come on, you alien monster!" he

yelled. "Give it your best shot!"

Then the alien did something Jake

wasn't expecting. It dropped the gun to

the floor with a clatter. It unsealed its

helmet with a hiss and slowly took it off.

Jake stared at a pair of soft, golden

eyes.

"No, human," said the alien. "I've seen too much death already."

Chapter 5
A Huge Trick

Jake dropped his knife. He had been

told by The Old Ones to hate the Krell, to

think of them as evil. But in all these

years of fighting, he had never been this

close to an alien. Not a living one,

anyway.

I was never sure they were evil, he

thought. *I know we've done just as many*

bad things in this war. And that face –

two eyes, a nose, a mouth ... it's not

much different from mine. She looks the

same age as me. And she must be a girl.

She couldn't be anything else with eyes

like that.

"So what now?" Jake said. "Are you letting me go?"

"If that is what you want," said the alien. Her voice was gentle, with a soft lilt to it. "But perhaps we could ... talk a little."

"What is there to talk about?" Jake said. *This is unreal,* he thought. *Am I dreaming? No, I can't be. The pain in my arm is far too real for that.*

"This stupid war," said the alien. She walked over to the window. Jake backed off, still wary of her. "I saw you running in the ruins," she said, "and I knew it was my duty to kill you. But I could not do it. I looked at you and I ... I wanted to know your name."

"My name?" said Jake, surprised. "Er ... it's Jake. What's yours?"

"I am Tala," she said. "Squad Leader of the Krell Night Scouts."

"I'm a Squad Leader too," said Jake. He almost told her the number of his unit, but then he stopped himself. *Maybe this is a set-up,* he thought. *Maybe it's just a cunning way to find out more about us. But there's something about her. Something open ...*

"I see you do not trust me yet," said Tala. "I do not blame you. There are many among the Krell who would find it hard to trust a human."

"But not you," said Jake, moving closer to her. "And you're dead right about this war. It is stupid. I don't even know how it started. Do you?"

Tala gave a sigh and looked out of the window. Jake did the same. Ruins stretched as far as they could see

beneath the silver moonlight. Some

patches still glowed blue. Far off the

fire-fight went on. Laser beams flickered

and sizzled.

"The Elders say our planet was dying,

and that we came here to seek help,"

Tala said. "They say you made us

welcome at first, but then some of you

turned on us, and we fought back. They

say that this is a fight for our survival. That you want to wipe us from your planet."

"Hey, that's what our Old Ones say too," said Jake. The pain in his arm was very bad now, and he was starting to feel hot and dizzy. "And I'll bet the only people doing the fighting on your side are the kids. It's all a huge trick, isn't it, Tala?"

Jake wanted to say a lot more, but the room seemed to be spinning. *I'm passing out*, he thought. Then his mind went dark and he fell ...

Chapter 6
Healing Time

He woke to find Tala kneeling beside

him. She pressed a metal disc against

his wound. There was a blue glow, and

Jake felt a wonderful wave of coolness

spread up through his arm and into the rest of his body.

"There, the medicine works on you," Tala said. "Our flesh is not so alien to each other. But you will still need some healing time."

Tala helped him up. He shook his head, took some deep breaths.

"Healing time ..." he said. "We could all do with some of that, Tala. Both sides, human and Krell. But first we need to stop the killing."

"Yes, but how?" said Tala. "We are children. The Elders will not listen to me. And they have much in common with your Old Ones."

"They won't live forever, though, will they?" said Jake, suddenly smiling. "And for now we can both tell the others. I'll tell my squad what you've told me. And you can tell your warriors that there are humans the Krell can trust. The truth will make it harder for us to kill each other."

Maybe I will be able to save the kids in my squad, thought Jake, *and many more like them. The only winner in a war like this is Death.*

"It is a good plan, Jake," said Tala, smiling. "A good plan indeed."

Jake smiled too, then held out his hand. Tala removed her glove, and took it. Jake could feel her skin smooth against his blood-stained palm.

"I must get back to my squad," said Jake. "Are they OK?"

"They are good fighters, Jake," said

Tala. "They are fine." Jake moved

towards the doorway, but Tala gently

held his arm. "Wait," she said. "I must

give the signal." She moved to the

landing and called out softly in her own

language.

It sounds like a waterfall, thought

Jake. *I wish I could speak her language*

as well as she speaks mine. Maybe one day I will.

Outside in the street Jake saw why Tala had stopped him going first. Two more Krell warriors stepped silently from the shadows. *She could have come in with back-up,* thought Jake. *I wouldn't have stood a chance.*

"So we have both learned something today, Jake," said Tala.

"You're right," said Jake. "Take care of yourself, Tala."

"I will, Jake," she said. "And you take care of yourself, too."

Just then Jake heard something behind him in the ruins. He looked around and saw people running their way, heard human voices.

"Hey, you'd ..." he said, turning to tell Tala and her warriors that they had better leave fast. But they had already slipped into the darkness.

"Jake, something crazy is going on," Tiny said, running up, the rest of the squad following. "The Krell had us pinned down, but suddenly they just vanished. Listen, I'm sorry we lost you. Are you OK?"

"Sure, Tiny," said Jake. "Come on,

let's get back to HQ."

He had an awful lot to do, and the

time to start was now.

Wolf
by
Tommy Donbavand

Adam didn't have much planned for this afternoon – head home from school, grab a snack, maybe play a video game before dinner. No way did he plan to grow some claws. Or *fur*. Or a *tail*. At this rate, Adam will be having his mom and dad *for* dinner. And they don't seem exactly surprised...

Mutant
by
Theresa Breslin

There was a strange smell in the room. It was coming from the air vents. As he watched, a wisp of smoke drifted out... Brad is always last to leave the Clone Unit. So when he forgets his watch and goes back the lab should be empty. But someone has other ideas...

Ninja: First Mission
by
Chris Bradford

When the Grandmaster sends Taka on a special mission, this is his last chance to prove himself. But the mission is dangerous. To fail is to die, and Taka has failed before...

The Dying Photo
by
Alan Gibbons

Their eyes were wide. Their mouths were open. They were screaming. When Jimmy first sees the man with the camera, he knows that something is very wrong. But no one will listen to him, not even when his mom and dad disappear. Can Jimmy track down the man again – and if he does, can he get his parents back?

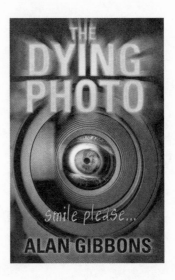

www.stokebooks.com